Katie Woo's

✳ Neighborhood ✳

The Best Baker

by Fran Manushkin

illustrated by Laura Zarrin

PICTURE WINDOW BOOKS
a capstone imprint

Katie Woo's Neighborhood is published by
Picture Window Books, an imprint of Capstone.
1710 Roe Crest Drive
North Mankato, Minnesota 56003
www.capstonepub.com

Text © 2020 by Fran Manushkin.
Illustrations © 2020 by Capstone.

Library of Congress Cataloging-in-Publication Data is available on the Library of Congress website.
ISBN: 978-1-5158-4813-4 (library binding)
ISBN: 978-1-5158-5873-7 (paperback)
ISBN: 978-1-5158-4817-2 (eBook PDF)

Summary: Katie and her friend Haley visit a bakery and learn how to bake yummy treats.

Designer: Bobbie Nuytten

Printed and bound in the USA.
PA100

Table of Contents

Katie's Neighborhood

Police

Library

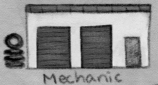
Mechanic

City
Hall

Grocery Store

Post Office

Chapter 1
Great Bakers

Katie and her friends were

eating cookies after school.

"I'm a great baker," said

Haley.

"Me too!" said Katie.

"Are you sure?" Katie's mom asked. "When you made chocolate cupcakes, they came out hard and salty."

"Oh," said Katie. "That's true."

"I made a birthday cake for my sister," said Haley. "But it fell apart. What a mess!"

Katie's mom asked Haley, "Doesn't your uncle own a bakery?"

"Yes," said Haley. "He works very hard. I'll ask him if he can teach us how to bake."

Surprise! Haley's uncle said he would show them.

Chapter 2
Sweet Dreams Bakery

On Saturday, Haley's
uncle Harry O'Hara met
them with a big smile and
two aprons.

"Welcome to the Sweet
Dreams Bakery!" he said.

Uncle Harry's kitchen was
neat and clean.

His cupcake and cake
pans were lined up in a row.

"Mom would love this,"
said Katie.

"I'll show you how to make chocolate cupcakes," said Uncle Harry. "Then I'll make a birthday cake."

"Yum!" said Haley.

"I'll say!" said Katie.

"Here is my cupcake recipe," said Uncle Harry. "It lists all the ingredients. See how carefully I measure them?"

Katie said, "Oops! When I made cupcakes, I just added lots of salt and chocolate powder."

"Not a good idea," said Uncle Harry.

Katie and Haley helped
pour the batter into frilly
cupcake cups.

"Try not to spill any," said
Uncle Harry. "Bakers hate
messes!"

"I'm setting the oven

to the perfect temperature

for cupcakes," said Uncle

Harry. "I also set a timer so

I know when the cupcakes

are ready."

"Now I need to bake a birthday cake," said Uncle Harry. "Ms. Malek ordered a big one to surprise her husband."

Uncle Harry sifted the flour. Then he added eggs and milk and other ingredients. He mixed them together.

Haley said, "Now I see the mistake I made baking my cake. I didn't mix my ingredients well. That's why my cake fell apart."

Chapter 3
Happy Bakers

After the cupcakes and cake were baked, it was time for frosting.

"This is the most fun," said Katie. "I love licking the spoon."

Uncle Harry began

yawning. "I was baking

all night," he explained.

"Bakers work long hours."

"I'll say!" said Katie.

"Thank you for showing us how to bake," said Katie. "From now on, I will measure well."

"And I will mix well," said Haley.

Katie's cupcakes came
out just right! She brought
them to JoJo and Pedro.
They loved them.

Haley's next cake was also perfect. It made her five brothers and sisters very happy.

But Harry O'Hara was the

happiest person of all.

Why?

Because he loved his

work. And so did everyone

else!

Glossary

baker (BAY-ker)—a person who cooks food, such as breads, cakes, and cookies

bakery (BAY-kuh-ree)—a place where baked goods, such as breads and cakes, are made and sold

frilly (FRIL-ee)—decorated with a ruffled strip of material or paper as a decoration

ingredients (in-GREE-dee-uhnts)—the items that something, such as a baked treat, are made from

sift (SIHFT)—in baking, to put a dry ingredient through a mesh-bottomed container to take out clumps and add air to the ingredient

temperature (TEM-pur-uh-chur)—the degree of hotness or coldness of something as shown by a thermometer

Katie's Questions

1. What traits make a good baker? Would you like to be a baker? Why or why not?

2. Explain why it is important to follow a recipe closely when you are baking something.

3. Imagine you are baking a cake for someone else. Write a paragraph to explain who you are baking for and why you chose them. Then draw a picture of the cake you would bake.

4. If you had your own bakery, what special things would you sell? Make a menu of the things you would sell at your bakery.

5. List five words to describe a cookie.

Katie Interviews a Baker

Katie: Hi, Mr. O'Hara! Thanks for talking to me about your bakery today.
Harry: Please just call me Harry! And I love talking about the bakery.

Katie: Okay, Harry! What do you like best about your job?
Harry: My favorite thing is creating birthday cakes! Whether I am covering a cake with frosting flowers or making a unicorn cake, I love knowing my cakes will make someone feel happy on their special day.

Katie: That's so nice! What is the trickiest cake you've ever made?
Harry: Once I made a cake that looked like a stand at the farmers market. I had to make all sorts of little vegetables out of something called fondant. It took forever! But it was beautiful when I was done.

Katie: I bet! And I'm sure it was tasty too! How did you learn to be a baker?
Harry: My grandma was my first teacher, and many of my recipes came from her. Then I worked in a bakery during high school. After I graduated, I went to a school that specializes in teaching people how to be professional bakers. But that's not all!

Katie: It's not?! What else?

Harry: Well, when I decided to open my own bakery, I took some business classes to learn how to best run my business.

Katie: One last question . . . tell me about your baker uniform please!

Harry: My jacket is called a chef jacket. It is comfortable, and I can move around easily in it. I wear a white one so you can't see flour on it. My pants are called chef trousers. They are comfortable too. And finally, comfortable shoes are a must! After all, I'm on my feet all day.

Katie: Hmm . . . well, since you are sitting down to talk to me anyway, maybe we should try one of your treats now.

Harry: Great idea, Katie!

About the Author

Fran Manushkin is the author of Katie Woo, the highly acclaimed fan-favorite early reader series, as well as the popular Pedro series. Her other books include *Happy in Our Skin, Baby, Come Out!* and

the best-selling board books *Big Girl Panties* and *Big Boy Underpants.* There is a real Katie Woo: Fran's great-niece, who doesn't get into trouble like the Katie in the books. Fran lives in New York City, three blocks from Central Park, where she can often be found bird-watching and daydreaming. She writes at her dining room table, without the help of her two naughty cats, Chaim and Goldy.

About the Illustrator

Laura spent her early childhood in the St. Louis, Missouri, area. There she explored creeks, woods, and attic closets, climbed trees, and dug for artifacts in the backyard, all in preparation for her future career as an archeologist. She never became one, however, because she realized she's much happier drawing in the comfort of her own home while watching TV. When she was twelve, her family moved to the Silicon Valley in California, where she still resides with her very logical husband and teen sons, and their illogical dog, Cody.